For George

Special thanks to Joan and Amy for being so supportive
over the many miles of my own artistic adventure.

First edition 2010

Library of Congress Cataloging-in-Publication Data

Harper, Jamie.
Miles to go / Jamie Harper. — 1st ed.
p. cm.
Summary: Although concerned about a broken horn, young Miles makes his way to preschool in his very own car, with Mom close at hand.
ISBN 978-0-7636-3598-5
[1. Automobile driving — Fiction.] I. Title.
PZ7.H23134Mil 2010
[E] — dc22 2009047411

10 11 12 13 14 15 CCP 10 9 8 7 6 5 4 3 2 1

Printed in Shenzhen, Guangdong, China

This book was typeset in Agenda.
The illustrations were done in block prints and mixed media collage, using watercolor, ink, and cut paper.

Candlewick Press
99 Dover Street
Somerville, Massachusetts 02144

visit us at www.candlewick.com

Miles
TO GO
JAMIE HARPER
CANDLEWICK PRESS

“Another day, another drive,” Miles says.

He packs up the car and climbs inside.
"Have to get to school!"

Miles puts on his
seat belt. CHECK.

Cranks the key.
CHECK.

Squeezes the horn.
UH-OH. Broken!
No time to fix it now.

"Gotta go!" says Miles.
He zigs around his
sister's trike.
He zags around his
brother's truck.

Pit stop.

“Fill ’er up,” says Miles.

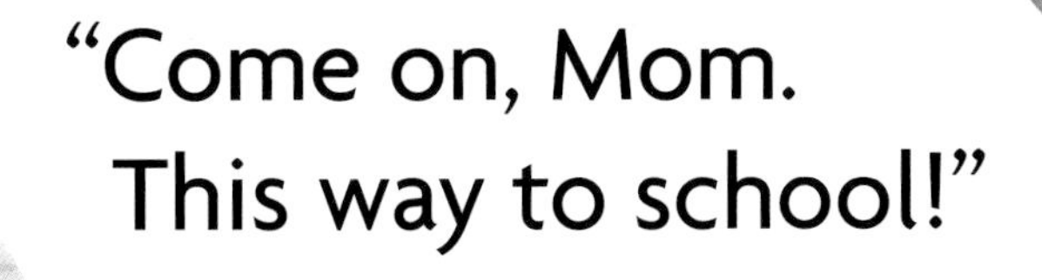

"Come on, Mom.
This way to school!"

BUMPITY-
BUMP

CLICKETY-CLUNK, CLICKETY-CLUNK

Miles speeds along the fence.

WOOF,
WOOF!

"BEEP, BEEP," says Miles.
"Sorry, Gus, no horn today."

DETOUR!
Mail the letters . . .

one at a time.

Oh, no. Trouble ahead.
Miles looks at the puddle.
He looks at his dusty car.

“Car wash!”

"Red light. C'mon, green."
Miles revs his engine.

GO!
Watch out for the
four-wheeler!
UH-OH! NO HORN!

ECH!

There’s the school bell.
“Bye, Mom, can’t be late.”

Miles zooms toward
the tunnel . . .

and swings into a space right next to Otto.

“Bad traffic!” says Otto.
“Broken horn!” says Miles.

OTTO

AMY

“Coming over later?”
asks Otto.

“Gotta take my car
to the shop,” says Miles.
“I’ll help,” says Otto.

Miles and Otto work all afternoon.

BEEP!
BEEP!

Soon they're back on track!

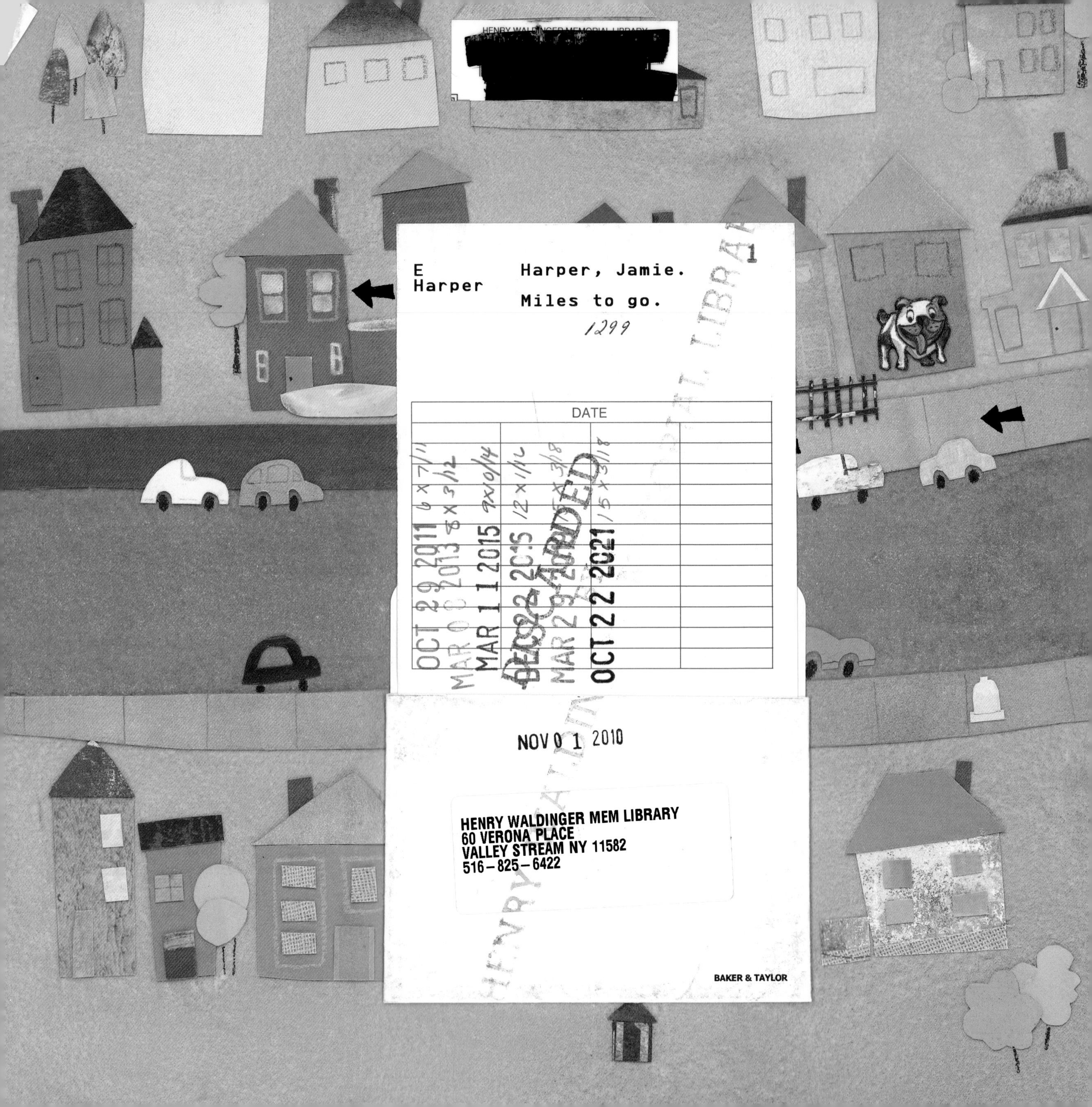
HENRY WALDINGER MEMORIAL LIBRARY
E
Harper
Harper, Jamie.
Miles to go.
1
DATE
OCT 29 2011
MAR 08 2013
MAR 11 2015
DEC 22 2015
MAR 29 2018
OCT 22 2021
DISCARDED
NOV 01 2010
HENRY WALDINGER MEM LIBRARY
60 VERONA PLACE
VALLEY STREAM NY 11582
516-825-6422
BAKER & TAYLOR